Schitt$ Creek

SIMPLY THE BEST QUOTES

NO-BRAINER BOOKS

Copyright © 2023 NO-BRAINER BOOKS
ISBN: 979-8387280320
All rights reserved.

Other books of this series:

The Office One Quote A Day - 979-8730711761
Friends: The One With The Quotes (Illustrated) - 979-8750745807
The Best Quotes from the Upside Down - 979-8366012294

"

EW, DAVID!

ALEXIS ROSE

"

GOSSIP IS THE DEVIL'S TELEPHONE. BEST TO JUST HANG UP.

MOIRA ROSE

> **YEAH I JUST FEEL LIKE THE WHOLE SESSION WAS RUSHED. LIKE, THERE WAS NO BACKLIGHTING, OR EMOTIONAL DIRECTION.**
>
> — DAVID ROSE

"

TALK TO THE HAND, SON. BECAUSE THE EARS ARE NO LONGER WORKING.

JOHNNY ROSE

"

I DON'T WANT TO BE TAKEN ADVANTAGE OF BECAUSE I'M OVERDRESSED.

JOHNNY ROSE

❝

THIS WINE IS AWFUL! GET ME ANOTHER GLASS.

MOIRA ROSE

"

I'M STARTING TO FEEL LIKE I'M TRAPPED IN AN AVRIL LAVIGNE LYRIC HERE.

DAVID ROSE

66

I WAS GIVING THEM A LITTLE PUP TALK

TED MULLENS

❝

MY CAR IS WORTH LESS THAN YOUR PANTS.

STEVIE BUDD

> I DO DRINK RED WINE. BUT I ALSO DRINK WHITE WINE. AND I'VE BEEN KNOWN TO SAMPLE THE OCCASIONAL ROSÉ. AND A COUPLE SUMMERS BACK I TRIED A MERLOT, THAT USED TO BE A CHARDONNAY. I LIKE THE WINE, AND NOT THE LABEL.

DAVID ROSE

66

I DON'T SKATE THROUGH LIFE. I WALK THROUGH LIFE... IN REALLY NICE SHOES.

ALEXIS ROSE

66

FALL OFF A BRIDGE, PLEASE.

DAVID ROSE

"

OH, IN CASE YOU WAKE UP IN A CHAIR WITH YOUR HANDS DUCT-TAPED TOGETHER, YOU CAN SNAP THE DUCT TAPE BY JUST RAISING YOUR HANDS OVER YOUR HEAD AND THEN BRINGING THEM DOWN REALLY HARD.

ALEXIS ROSE

66

WHO PUT A PICTURE OF A GHOST ON MY DESK?

MOIRA ROSE

❝

TWEET US ON FACEBOOK!

JOHNNY ROSE

❝

WHAT YOU DID WAS IMPULSIVE, CAPRICIOUS, AND MELODRAMATIC. BUT, IT WAS ALSO WRONG.

MOIRA ROSE

"

ROSE APOTHECARY. YOU KNOW, IT'S JUST PRETENTIOUS ENOUGH.

PATRICK BREWER

> "WELL, IF I FIND OUT THAT YOU'RE ACCUSING ME OF DOING SOMETHING I DIDN'T DO, THEN I'M GOING TO ACCUSE YOU OF MAKING FALSE ACCUSATIONS."

— ROLAND SCHITT

"

DAVID, WILL YOU PLEASE GIVE ME A HUG?

ALEXIS ROSE

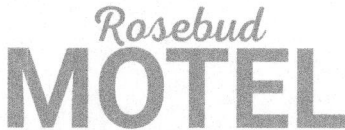

"

I DIDN'T GO MISSING, DAVID. THE FBI KNEW WHERE I WAS THE ENTIRE TIME!

ALEXIS ROSE

WHERE IS BÉBÉS CHAMBER?

MOIRA ROSE

"

THIS ISN'T SAY YES TO THE DRESS, PRINCESS. ORANGE IS THE NEW ORANGE.

RONNIE

"

I'M ONLY DOING THIS BECAUSE YOU CALLED ME RUDE, AND I TAKE THAT AS A COMPLIMENT.

STEVIE BUDD

"

IF YOU'RE LOOKING FOR AN ASS TO KISS, IT'S MINE.

ROLAND SCHITT

❝

YOU'RE MY MARIAH CAREY.

PATRICK BREWER

> I'VE BEEN WAITING FOR THIS MOMENT. APPARENTLY, IF THEY CALL YOUR NUMBER, YOU GET TO STAND IN FRONT OF A JUDGE. I FEEL LIKE I'M ON THE VOICE!

— JOCELYN SCHITT

66

DAVID, THE PEDALS MAKE IT MOVE MORE.

ALEXIS ROSE

"

OH, IT'S ALWAYS JUST A COLD, JOHN- UNTIL IT'S FULL-BLOWN TYPHOID!

MOIRA ROSE

❝

COME TASTE THE DIFFERENCE GOOD FRUIT CAN MAKE IN YOUR WINE. YOU'LL REMEMBER THE EXPERIENCE AND YOU'LL REMEMBER THE NAME.

MOIRA ROSE

"

EXCUSE ME, I HAVEN'T BEDAZZLED ANYTHING SINCE I WAS 22.

DAVID ROSE

>

I COULD NOT BE MORE AT ONE WITH NATURE. I DO COACHELLA EVERY YEAR.

DAVID ROSE

> YOU'D HAVE SAID 'WOW, ALEXIS! I'M THINKING ABOUT SHAVING MY BEARD.' AND THEN I WOULD'VE SAID 'MMH…NO MUTT, I DON'T THINK THAT THAT'S THE RIGHT JOURNEY FOR YOU AT THIS POINT IN TIME.'

ALEXIS ROSE

❝

YOU'D THINK THERE'D BE MORE OF A MARKET FOR OVERSIZED PAINTINGS OF OTHER PEOPLE'S FAMILIES.

STEVIE BUDD

66

A LITTLE BIT ALEXIS!

ALEXIS ROSE

> **YOU KNOW WHAT, DAVID? YOU GET MURDERED FIRST FOR ONCE.**
>
> — ALEXIS ROSE

Rosebud **MOTEL**

> # ❝
>
> I PLAN ON POPPING A PILL, CRYING A BIT, AND FALLING ASLEEP EARLY.
>
> — DAVID ROSE

Rosebud MOTEL

> # YOU JUST FOLD IT IN.
>
> — MOIRA ROSE

Rosebud MOTEL

"

WELL, THIS TOWN IS VERY SCREAMNASTIC.

JOHNNY ROSE

Rosebud
MOTEL

> **I HAVE NEVER HEARD SOMEONE SAY SO MANY WRONG THINGS, ONE AFTER THE OTHER, CONSECUTIVELY, IN A ROW.**
>
> DAVID ROSE

Rosebud **MOTEL**

> **WHAT NOW? DO I LEAVE EVERYTHING BEHIND AND MOVE TO SOME RANDOM ISLAND TO BE WITH THE LOVE OF MY LIFE? BECAUSE I DID THAT WITH HARRY STYLES IN ENGLAND AND IT WAS, LIKE, TOO RAINY.**

— ALEXIS ROSE

Rosebud **MOTEL**

66

DAVID, I'M HUNGRY. I'M A HUNGRY HUNGRY HIPPO!

PATRICK BREWER

Rosebud MOTEL

"

EVERYONE SHUT UP! RONNIE, THROW THE THING!

DAVID ROSE

Rosebud **MOTEL**

"

LIKE BEYONCE, I EXCEL AS A SOLO ARTIST.

DAVID ROSE

Rosebud
MOTEL

> IS THERE, LIKE, A TEXAS CHAINSAW MOVIE BEING FILMED OUT THERE THAT I'M NOT AWARE OF?

DAVID ROSE

"

I WILL NOT FEEL SHAME ABOUT THE MALL PRETZELS.

DAVID ROSE

Rosebud MOTEL

> **YOU MIGHT WANT TO RETHINK THE NIGHTGOWN FIRST. THERE'S A WHOLE EBENEZER SCROOGE THING HAPPENING. MY BEST TO BOB CRATCHET.**
>
> DAVID ROSE

Rosebud MOTEL

"

YOU SMELL VERY FLAMMABLE RIGHT NOW.

DAVID ROSE

Rosebud
MOTEL

> JUST THINK OF THEM AS TINY LITTLE ROOMMATES WHOSE TINY LITTLE POOPS YOU GET TO CLEAN UP.

ALEXIS ROSE

Rosebud
MOTEL

"

OH, I'D KILL FOR A GOOD COMA RIGHT NOW.

MOIRA ROSE

Rosebud
MOTEL

> FUNKY IS A NEON T-SHIRT YOU BUY AT AN AIRPORT GIFT SHOP NEXT TO A BEJEWELED IPHONE CASE. THIS IS LUXURY.

DAVID ROSE

Rosebud
MOTEL

> # THIS PLACE IS ALMOST CHARMING. VERY RUSTIC COTTAGE... I WAS HALF EXPECTING EARLY UNABOMBER.
>
> — MOIRA ROSE

Rosebud MOTEL

"

WE JUST NEED A BODY.

PATRICK BREWER

Rosebud MOTEL

"

I DON'T WANT TO BRAG, BUT US WEEKLY ONCE DESCRIBED ME AS 'UP FOR ANYTHING.

ALEXIS ROSE

Rosebud
MOTEL

"

WHY AM I GETTING BOOED?

JOHNNY ROSE

Rosebud MOTEL

> I AM SUDDENLY OVERWHELMED WITH REGRET. IT'S A NEW FEELING FOR ME, AND I DON'T FIND IT AT ALL PLEASURABLE.

— MOIRA ROSE

Rosebud **MOTEL**

"

I WON'T WEAR ANYTHING WITH AN ADHESIVE BACKING.

MOIRA ROSE

Rosebud MOTEL

>

IF THOSE BUNNIES FEEL EXPLOITED EVEN A LITTLE BIT, I AM PULLING THE PLUG.

TED MULLENS

Rosebud **MOTEL**

"

HASHTAG. IS THAT TWO WORDS?

JOHNNY ROSE

Rosebud MOTEL

> # DO I WEAR A FRINGED VEST? OR MORE IMPORTANTLY, DO I WEAR ANYTHING UNDER IT?

PATRICK BREWER

Rosebud
MOTEL

❝

YOU'RE NOT THE ONLY ONE WITH AN ONLINE PRESENCE.

JOHNNY ROSE

Rosebud MOTEL

> # ❝
>
> HOW MERCURIAL IS LIFE. WE ALL IMAGINE BEING CARRIED FROM THE ASHES BY THE GODDESS ARTEMIS, AND HERE I GET A BALATRON FROM BARNUM & BAILEY.
>
> — MOIRA ROSE

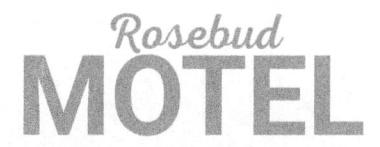

Rosebud MOTEL

"

MY SON IS PANSEXUAL.

JOHNNY ROSE

Rosebud **MOTEL**

> **IF AIRPLANE SAFETY VIDEOS HAVE TAUGHT ME ANYTHING, DAVID, IT'S THAT A MOTHER PUTS HER OWN MASK ON FIRST.**
>
> — MOIRA ROSE

Rosebud MOTEL

> HONESTLY, TWY? IX-NAY ON THE ONG- SAY BECAUSE I TRIED IT ONCE, AND THE GUY RIPPED THE GUITAR OUT OF MY HANDS AND HE JUST STARTED SMASHING IT ON THE GROUND. GRANTED, I AM TONE DEAF, AND HE WAS A SUPER ANGRY MARINE. BUT...

ALEXIS ROSE

Rosebud **MOTEL**

66

STOP DOING THAT WITH YOUR FACE.

ALEXIS ROSE

Rosebud
MOTEL

> HE LOVES EVERYONE. MEN, WOMEN, WOMEN WHO BECOME MEN, MEN WHO BECOME WOMEN. I'M HIS FATHER, AND I ALWAYS WANTED HIS LIFE TO BE EASY. BUT, YOU KNOW, JUST PICK ONE GENDER, AND MAYBE, MAYBE EVERYTHING WOULD'VE BEEN LESS CONFUSING.

— JOHNNY ROSE

Rosebud MOTEL

> **I'D REALLY LIKE YOU TO SING AT MY COUSIN'S FUNERAL. SHE'S NOT DEAD, BUT SHE'S BEEN COUGHING A LOT LATELY.**
>
> — ROLAND SCHITT

Rosebud **MOTEL**

> ALLOW ME TO OFFER SOME ADVICE. TAKE A THOUSAND NAKED PICTURES OF YOURSELF NOW. YOU MAY CURRENTLY THINK, 'OH, I'M TOO SPOOKY,' OR 'NOBODY WANTS TO SEE THESE TINY BOOBIES,' BUT BELIEVE ME: ONE DAY YOU WILL LOOK AT THOSE PHOTOS WITH MUCH KINDER EYES AND SAY, 'DEAR GOD, I WAS A BEAUTIFUL THING!

— MOIRA ROSE

Rosebud **MOTEL**

❝

OK, WELL, MOVIES AREN'T ALWAYS RIGHT, ALL RIGHT? YOU'LL LEARN THAT LATER IN LIFE.

DAVID ROSE

Rosebud MOTEL

> I KNOW ALL ABOUT BEING LEFT IN THE LURCH FOR A FUNDRAISER. EVA LONGORIA AND I WERE SUPPOSED TO PERFORM OUR VENTRILOQUIST ACT FOR THE EVERYBODY NOSE BENEFIT FOR JUVENILE RHINOPLASTY WHEN SHE SUDDENLY DROPS OUT DUE TO EXHAUSTION. I HAD TO BE BOTH PUPPET AND PUPPETEER!

— MOIRA ROSE

Rosebud
MOTEL

"

SHE SORT OF FADES INTO THE BACKGROUND AFTER A WHILE. YOU KNOW, LIKE A SMOKE ALARM.

DAVID ROSE

Rosebud **MOTEL**

> DO I HAVE TO REMIND YOU OF THE TIME THAT I WAS TAKEN HOSTAGE ON DAVID GEFFEN'S YACHT BY SOMALI PIRATES FOR A WEEK, AND NOBODY ANSWERED MY TEXTS?

— ALEXIS ROSE

Rosebud MOTEL

> **"**

I WOULD BE PLEASED TO RSVP AS PENDING.

MOIRA ROSE

Rosebud
MOTEL

> **WELL, YOU KNOW, JOHNNY, WHEN IT COMES TO MATTERS OF THE HEART, WE CAN'T TELL OUR KIDS WHO TO LOVE. WHO SAID THAT?**
>
> — ROLAND SCHITT

Rosebud **MOTEL**

"

FEAR NOT, SHE HATH RISEN!

MOIRA ROSE

Rosebud MOTEL

>

I AM SUFFERING
ROMANTICALLY
RIGHT NOW.

DAVID ROSE

Rosebud
MOTEL

> I DON'T KNOW WHY YOU DIDN'T ASK ME FIRST, DAVID. I HAVE MY LICENSE IN SEVEN DIFFERENT COUNTRIES AND I HAVE MY F CLASS.

— ALEXIS ROSE

Rosebud MOTEL

"

I'M A DELIGHTFUL HALF-HALF SITUATION!

DAVID ROSE

Rosebud **MOTEL**

"

IT'S A LIST OF BUZZFEED'S MOST MOTIVATIONAL QUOTES FOR GIRL BOSSES UNDER THIRTY.

ALEXIS ROSE

Rosebud
MOTEL

>

I WENT ON A BLIND DATE TO BALI WITH LEO, SO I'M PRETTY SURE IT'LL BE FINE.

ALEXIS ROSE

Rosebud MOTEL

> YOU KNOW, BEING APPROACHABLE ISN'T THAT IMPORTANT, ANYWAY. THE QUEEN HASN'T SMILED SINCE THE '70S AND HER BIRTHDAYS ARE STILL VERY WELL ATTENDED.

DAVID ROSE

Rosebud **MOTEL**

> NO MATTER WHAT ANYONE SAYS, YOU WILL ALWAYS BE OUR FIRST DAD.

DAVID ROSE

Rosebud MOTEL

> I HAVE MY OWN HOLIDAY TRADITION. IT'S LIKE THE 12 DAYS OF CHRISTMAS, BUT IT'S ONE DAY WITH 12 BOTTLES OF WINE.

STEVIE BUDD

Rosebud **MOTEL**

"

THE INTERNET IS A BREEDING GROUND FOR FREAKS.

DAVID ROSE

Rosebud
MOTEL

"

I GOT THESE ON A CLEARANCE RACK AT TARGET.

STEVIE BUDD

Rosebud
MOTEL

> MY NAME IS ALEXIS, AND YES, I DID NOT FINISH HIGH SCHOOL. UM, IT'S THIS LONG, BORING STORY INVOLVING A YACHT, AND A FAMOUS SOCCER PLAYER, AND LIKE A TON OF MUSHROOMS.

— ALEXIS ROSE

Rosebud MOTEL

"

WE'RE DRINKING TO ME NOT BECOMING AN ALCOHOLIC.

STEVIE BUDD

Rosebud
MOTEL

"

THERE'S NOTHING HERE BUT HOT SINGLES IN MY AREA.

MOIRA ROSE

Rosebud
MOTEL

"

I WASN'T IN REHAB: I WAS AT REHAB, VISITING STAVROS.

ALEXIS ROSE

Rosebud MOTEL

> **THE IDEA OF ME LIFE COACHING ANOTHER HUMAN BEING SHOULD SCARE YOU... A LOT.**
>
> — DAVID ROSE

Rosebud **MOTEL**

"

BUT PEOPLE LOVE EXTREME VANITY... AND THEY LOVE PUPPIES!

ALEXIS ROSE

Rosebud
MOTEL

> As if I didn't see this coming. He's broken up with me five times already. Like there was that time that he never met me in Rio. And remember that time when he gave me his ex-wife's engagement ring? And then there was that time last summer when he left his molly in my glove department and then I got arrested.

— ALEXIS ROSE

Rosebud MOTEL

"

I GOT THESE AT A SHOWROOM IN PARIS.

DAVID ROSE

Rosebud MOTEL

> OK, YEAH, I STILL ACTUALLY HAD A FEW MORE VERSES. AND IN THE LAST VERSE, I REALLY GET TO SHOWCASE MY RANGE.

ALEXIS ROSE

Rosebud MOTEL

"

YOU DO REALIZE I'M A PROFESSIONAL VOCALIST?

MOIRA ROSE

Rosebud
MOTEL

> **MY SON LIVES IN A BARN IN THE WOODS, BY CHOICE. HE COULD BE THE NEXT MAYOR OF THIS TOWN IF HE WANTED IT.**

ROLAND SCHITT

Rosebud
MOTEL

"

SOMEONE BROUGHT ROOM TEMPERATURE VODKA.

DAVID ROSE

Rosebud
MOTEL

> OH, LOOK AT DAVID. SMART ENOUGH TO GET THAT JOKE, BUT NOT SMART ENOUGH TO STOP WEARING SWEATERS IN THE MIDDLE OF THE SUMMER.

— JOHNNY ROSE

Rosebud **MOTEL**

"

I LIKE THE WINE AND NOT THE LABEL.

DAVID ROSE

Rosebud
MOTEL

> ANYWAY, SO YOU'VE BEEN BURNED A COUPLE TIMES. UM, HAVE WE MET? I'VE BEEN BURNED SO MANY TIMES I'M LIKE THE HUMAN EQUIVALENT OF THE INSIDE OF A ROASTED MARSHMALLOW.

DAVID ROSE

Rosebud **MOTEL**

FOLD IN THE CHEESE.

DAVID ROSE

Rosebud MOTEL

"

DAVID, YOU HAVE TO STOP WATCHING NOTTING HILL. IT'S NOT HELPFUL FOR OUR RELATIONSHIP.

PATRICK BREWER

Rosebud
MOTEL

"

EAT GLASS.

DAVID ROSE

Rosebud MOTEL

"

I MISS BEING SURROUNDED BY LOOSE ACQUAINTANCES WHO THINK I'M FUNNY AND SMART AND CHARMING.

ALEXIS ROSE

Rosebud
MOTEL

"

JUST WATCH A SEASON OF GIRLS AND DO THE OPPOSITE.

DAVID ROSE

Rosebud
MOTEL

> "I'VE SPENT MOST OF MY LIFE NOT KNOWING WHAT RIGHT WAS SUPPOSED TO FEEL LIKE AND THEN I MET YOU AND EVERYTHING CHANGED. YOU MAKE ME FEEL RIGHT.

PATRICK BREWER

Rosebud **MOTEL**

> LET'S GO. I'VE HAD ENOUGH WAKING HOURS FOR ONE DAY.

MOIRA ROSE

Rosebud MOTEL

"

I'M TRYING VERY HARD NOT TO CONNECT WITH PEOPLE RIGHT NOW.

DAVID ROSE

Rosebud
MOTEL

> POLITICS 101. JOHN. WHEN YOU HAVE LIMITED RESOURCES, YOUR BEST COURSE OF ACTION IS TO CREATE A STIR. IT'S EXCITING. IT'S FUN. IT'S LIKE THAT EPISODE OF SUNRISE BAY WHEN I STOLE MY OWN BEBE.

— MOIRA ROSE

Rosebud **MOTEL**

> **WAIT, ONE PIZZA? WHAT IS THIS? LES MIS?**
>
> DAVID ROSE

Rosebud MOTEL